Russell's Secret

by Johanna Hurwitz
illustrated by Heather Maione

HarperCollinsPublishers

This story is adapted from the chapter "Why Russell Was Late"
in the book *Rip-Roaring Russell*.

Russell's Secret
Text copyright © 2001 by Johanna Hurwitz
Illustrations copyright © 2001 by Heather Maione
Printed in the U.S.A. All rights reserved.
www.harperchildrens.com

Library of Congress Cataloging-in-Publication Data
Hurwitz, Johanna.
Russell's secret / by Johanna Hurwitz ; illustrated by Heather Maione.
p.   cm.
Summary: When Russell decides to stay home from nursery school and
be a baby just like his new sister, he discovers that being treated like a baby
when you are a big boy is no fun at all.
ISBN 0-688-17574-0 — ISBN 0-688-17575-9 (lib. bdg.)
[1. Babies—Fiction.   2. Brothers and sisters—Fiction.]   I. Maione,
Heather Harms, ill.   II. Title.
PZ7.H9574 Rus   2001   00-33577
[E]—dc21   CIP
                                                                           AC

Typography by Stephanie Bart-Horvath
1   2   3   4   5   6   7   8   9   10
❖
First Edition

It's no secret:
I love
Ethan & Juliet.
—J.H.

For my mother, Sylvia Ingram
—H.M.

Five days a week Russell Michaels went to the Sunshine Nursery School. But one Monday morning he woke up and decided he didn't want to go to school.

"I want to stay home," he whined when his mother started to help him get dressed.

"Don't be silly," said his mother. "Of course you want to go to school."

"I *don't* want to go to school!" said Russell. He wasn't sure why. He just wanted to stay home the way he had when he was little, before his baby sister, Elisa, was born.

"Aren't you feeling well?" asked his mother. She felt his forehead. "Let me see your tongue."

Russell opened his mouth and stuck out his tongue.

"Your head is cool, and your tongue is red. You're in fine shape," his mother diagnosed.

"I don't care," insisted Russell. "I want to stay home."

"Only little babies like Elisa stay home," said Russell's mother. "You're a big boy. You're four years old."

"I want to be a baby!" shouted Russell. He lay down on the floor and began kicking his feet and crying. He was acting just like a baby.

In the next room Elisa began crying too. With two children crying, it was very noisy at Russell's home.

"All right," shouted Russell's mother to her son. "If you want to be a baby, you can stay home and be a baby today."

Russell stopped crying at once and felt very happy. He knew he was going to have such a good time being a baby all day long.

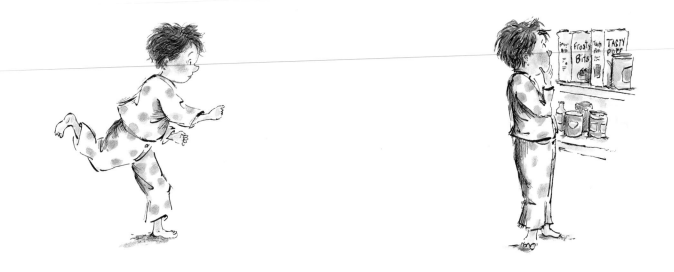

He ran right into the kitchen. While he was still deciding between crispy Frosty Bits and crunchy Tasty Pops, his mother came into the kitchen. She put Elisa into her high chair. Then she placed a steaming bowl in front of Russell.

"Yuck!" said Russell, making a face. "What is this?"

"It's nutritious rice cereal. Elisa eats it every morning unless she has hot oatmeal instead."

"I don't want any," said Russell, pushing the bowl away.

Russell's mother put a spoonful of the hot cereal inside his mouth. The cereal was awful, and Russell was about to spit it out. Then he remembered that whenever Elisa did that, their mother managed to shovel the food right back inside her mouth again. So he swallowed and held his mouth firmly shut. That one spoonful was all he had for breakfast.

Russell left the kitchen and ran into the living room. He turned on the television. It would be fun to see all the good programs that he had to miss every day when he went to school.

"Oh no!" his mother said. She turned off the TV.

"I want to watch TV," said Russell.

"I'm sorry. Babies don't watch television," he was told.

Russell didn't like that one bit. But he decided it was still more fun to stay home and be a baby than to go to school.

So he went to his room to find something to play with. He took
his box of Legos off the shelf and began building with them.

"You naughty boy!" his mother called out when she saw
what he was doing. "You can't play with such tiny pieces. You
might swallow them."

"I always play with Legos and I never put them in my mouth," Russell protested.

"But now you're being a baby," his mother reminded him as she took the Legos away. "Babies always put little things inside their mouths."

"Well, what can I do?" Russell wanted to know.

"Since you are my other baby today, you'd better come with me," his mother decided. "This is how we keep babies out of mischief." She helped Russell climb inside Elisa's playpen.

"Now you stay there and play," she told him.

Elisa sat in one corner of the playpen and smiled at her brother. She seemed to think his being there was a big joke.

Since a playpen is a little like a cage, he pretended that the two of them were lions at the zoo. Then he pretended that they were astronauts inside a space capsule.

But the playpen was small and cramped, and Elisa didn't really know how to play at all. Russell got bored. He looked around. There were only some rubber baby toys inside the playpen. He didn't want to play with them.

He climbed out of the playpen and went to find his mother.

She was vacuuming in the next room.

"I'm hungry," Russell complained over the noise of the vacuum cleaner.

"I'm not surprised," his mother said. "You didn't have very much for breakfast. Would you like a snack?"

"Oh yes," said Russell, nodding eagerly.

"I'll fix something," his mother told him. She took some milk and put it in a pan and warmed it. Next she poured the milk into a bottle. On top of the bottle she put a nipple. Then she handed it to Russell.

Russell thought it would be fun to drink from a baby bottle the way Elisa did. But only a tiny squirt of milk came out of the nipple. Russell didn't like the taste of it either.

"Yuck!" he said. "I don't like hot milk."

"Hot milk is just like hot cocoa without the chocolate flavoring," said his mother.

"But I don't like plain hot milk. I like the chocolate flavoring," Russell told her.

"Babies don't get chocolate," she replied.

"What happens next?" asked Russell. He seemed to have forgotten so many things about being a baby.

"Next it will be time for your nap," his mother announced.

"*Nap?* I just woke up," Russell reminded his mother. "I don't want to take a nap."

"Babies always have a nap," his mother said. "Elisa has a nap every morning."

"What happens after nap time?" Russell wanted to know.

"After nap time, it will be lunchtime."

"Oh, good," said Russell, feeling relieved. By now he was really getting hungry.

"What's for lunch today?"

His mother thought for a minute. "I think I'll make some nice mashed carrots and mashed peas. And for dessert I'm going to fix Elisa's favorite—mashed bananas. It was your favorite when you were a baby too."

"Yuck!" said Russell, making a face. "That's awful. It's terrible being a baby. I don't like being a baby at all."

"Oh, Russell," his mother said, bending down to give him a hug. "It's fun to be a baby when you *are* a baby. It's just not so much fun to be a baby when you're a big boy."

Suddenly Russell had an idea. "Could I go to school?" he asked.
"Well," said his mother, looking at her watch. "It's getting late, but if you hurry you could still go to school today."

Russell went into his bedroom to get his clothing because he had been wearing his pajamas all this time.

Russell's mother put some clothes on Elisa so they could take him to school.

She also put together a little snack for Russell to eat on the
way to school so he wouldn't be hungry.

She gave him two oatmeal cookies, nice and crunchy, and a
little box of raisins, nice and chewy. Nothing mashed.

When he got to school, everyone asked, "Russell, why are you so late?"

For a moment Russell didn't say anything. Then he gave his answer: "It's a secret," he told them.